No Ordinary Mouse

The Tale of Despereaux™

No Ordinary Mouse

The Tale of Despereaux

Based on the motion picture screenplay by Gary Ross
Based on the book by Kate DiCamillo

CANDLEWICK PRESS

First edition 2008

Library of Congress Cataloging-in-Publication Data is available.
Library of Congress Catalog Card Number 2008927242
ISBN 978-0-7636-4078-1

2 4 6 8 10 9 7 5 3 1

Printed in the United States of America

This book was typeset in Garamond Ludlow.
The artwork was created digitally.

Candlewick Press
99 Dover Street
Somerville, Massachusetts 02144

visit us at www.candlewick.com

Contents

Chapter One
No Ordinary Mouse

Once upon a time, in the Kingdom of Dor, a mouse was born. His name was Despereaux Tilling.

From the beginning, Despereaux looked and acted differently from other mice.

"He's so puny," his older brother, Furlough, said. "And look at those big ears!"

As he grew, Despereaux remained small, even for a mouse. But in his own mind, he was a giant—brave and strong.

He didn't cower and he didn't scurry. He set off mousetraps for fun.

In school, he drew a picture of a cat
and named it Fluffy!

Despereaux's parents
wanted him to act more
like the other mice, so
they asked Furlough to
show him how to behave.

Furlough took Despereaux to the royal library. It was filled with hundreds of books. Furlough started to munch on one.

"The glue is all right, but it's the pages that taste best," he said.

But Despereaux wasn't listening. He was reading!

"You're not supposed to *read* the book, Despereaux. You're supposed to *eat* it!" his brother reminded him. "It's a rule."

But Despereaux kept reading. He read about honor and courage, and about a sad princess and the brave knight who sets out to rescue her.

One day, the Mouse Council found him reading. They were very angry that he had broken their rules, so they brought him to trial.

"You shall be exiled — alone — into the dungeons of Dor," they told him.

Despereaux was banished. For the first time in his life, he felt afraid.

Little did he know that this was the beginning of a great adventure!

Chapter Two
An Unlikely Friendship

Before he was banished, Despereaux used to wonder what was beyond the mouse village.

The other mice, who were afraid of everything, trembled when Despereaux asked about the dungeon.

"There are rats down there," one of the mice had told him. But Despereaux was still curious.

Somewhere, there has to be someone out there like me, Despereaux thought.

And there was someone out there like him—but he was a rat. His name was Roscuro.

Roscuro was a sailor when he first came to Dor, but then he accidentally fell into the queen's soup bowl and scared her. The palace guards chased Roscuro to the dungeon, where he had remained ever since.

There Roscuro met Botticelli, the
leader of the rats. He taught Roscuro how
to act like the other rats in the dungeon.
But Roscuro was not
like them. He did not
like the darkness and the
dirty dungeon where they
lived. He did not like the
rats' songs and dances.

"Stinky, dark and foul
and rotting, oozing sores and
blood that's clotting. Mmm!
Delicious! Hits the spot!
It's great to be a rat!"
the other rats sang.

When Despereaux was banished to
the dungeon, it was Roscuro who saved
his life. The other rats wanted to feed him
to a cat!

But Roscuro had heard Despereaux
talking about a princess. He wanted to
know more, so he rescued
Despereaux and brought
him to his secret nook.

"Tell me the
rest of that story,"
Roscuro said.
"The one about
the princess."

So Despereaux told him all about the
princess, and Roscuro listened.

And that's how a rat and a mouse
became friends.

Chapter Three
The Princess and the Quest

The princess Despereaux had met was named Pea, and she was very sad.

Before he was banished, Despereaux had seen the princess looking out her window and crying.

"Why are you crying?" he asked her.

The princess looked around, but she didn't see anyone.

"Down here," Despereaux said.

Finally the princess saw him. "Are you a rat?" she asked.

"I am a gentleman," Despereaux said as he bowed to the princess.

Despereaux explained that he was reading a story about a sad princess who lived in a castle, just like Pea.

Pea asked him to tell her how the story ended.

Despereaux promised the princess that he would finish reading the story and return.

He couldn't wait to see Princess Pea again. Despereaux was so excited that he told Furlough all about her, even though it was against mouse rules to talk to a human.

But before he could return to finish
the story, Despereaux was banished to
the dungeon. There he heard a familiar
voice calling for help. It was Pea! She had
been kidnapped and taken down to the
dungeon as well.

I have to rescue her, Despereaux thought. *It will be my quest.* He remembered the story he had been reading in the library.

"Chivalry! Bravery! Honor!" he repeated. He knew that he had to save the princess, but he couldn't do it alone.

With help from his friend Roscuro
and a magical knight made of vegetables,
Despereaux was able to defeat the rats and
save the princess.

Despereaux had fulfilled his quest.

So, you could say that everyone lived happily ever after . . . but what is fun about that?

The End